'ALE TERROR
GOES BEFORE
HIM, DEATH
AND
DEVASTATION
FOLLOW
AFTER!'

MARK TWAIN
Born 1835, Florida, Missouri
Died 1910, Redding, Connecticut

PENGUIN CLASSICS

UK | USA | Canada | Ireland | Australia
India | New Zealand | South Africa

Penguin Classics is part of the Penguin Random House group of companies
whose addresses can be found at global.penguinrandomhouse.com.

This selection published in Penguin Classics 2016

001

Set in 9.5/13 pt Baskerville 10 Pro
Typeset by Jouve (UK), Milton Keynes
Printed in Great Britain by Clays Ltd, St Ives plc

A CIP catalogue record for this book is available from the British Library

ISBN: 978–0–241–25174–4

www.greenpenguin.co.uk

Penguin Random House is committed to a
sustainable future for our business, our readers
and our planet. This book is made from Forest
Stewardship Council® certified paper.

MARK TWAIN

The Stolen White Elephant

PENGUIN BOOKS

Contents

The Stolen White Elephant

1

The following curious history was related to me by a chance railway acquaintance. He was a gentleman more than seventy years of age, and his thoroughly good and gentle face and earnest and sincere manner imprinted the unmistakable stamp of truth upon every statement which fell from his lips. He said:

You know in what reverence the royal white elephant of Siam is held by the people of that country. You know it is sacred to kings, only kings may possess it, and that it is indeed in a measure even superior to kings, since it receives not merely honour but worship. Very well; five years ago, when the troubles concerning the frontier line arose between Great Britain and Siam, it was presently manifest that Siam had been in the wrong. Therefore every reparation was quickly made, and the British representative stated that he was satisfied and the past should be forgotten. This greatly relieved the King of Siam, and partly as a token of gratitude, but partly also, perhaps, to wipe out any little remaining vestige of unpleasantness which England might feel toward him, he wished to send the Queen a present – the sole sure way of propitiating an enemy, according to Oriental ideas. This present ought not only to be a royal one, but transcendently royal. Wherefore, what offering could be so meet as that of a white elephant? My position in the Indian civil service was such that I was deemed peculiarly worthy of the honour of conveying the present to her Majesty. A ship was fitted out for me and my servants and the officers and attendants of the elephant, and in due time I arrived in New York harbour and placed my royal charge in admirable quarters in Jersey City. It was necessary to remain awhile in order to recruit the animal's health before resuming the voyage.

All went well during a fortnight – then my calamities began. The white elephant was stolen! I was called up at dead of night and informed of this fearful misfortune. For some moments I was beside myself with terror and anxiety; I was helpless. Then I grew calmer and collected my faculties. I soon saw my course – for indeed there was but the one course for an intelligent man to pursue. Late as it was, I flew to New York and got a policeman to conduct me to the headquarters of the detective force. Fortunately I arrived in time, though the chief of the force, the celebrated Inspector Blunt, was just on the point of leaving for his home. He was a man of middle size and compact frame, and when he was thinking deeply he had a way of knitting his brows and tapping his forehead reflectively with his finger, which impressed you at once with the conviction that you stood in the presence of a person of no common order. The very sight of him gave me confidence and made me hopeful. I stated my errand. It did not flurry him in the least; it had no more visible effect upon his iron self-possession than if I had told him somebody had stolen my dog. He motioned me to a seat, and said calmly, 'Allow me to think a moment, please.'

So saying, he sat down at his office table and leaned his head upon his hand. Several clerks were at work at the other end of the room; the scratching of their pens was all the sound I heard during the next six or seven minutes. Meantime the inspector sat there, buried in thought. Finally he raised his head, and there was that in the firm lines of his face which showed me that his brain had done its work and his plan was made. Said he – and his voice was low and impressive, 'This is no ordinary case. Every step must be warily taken; each step must be made sure before the next is ventured. And secrecy must be observed – secrecy profound and absolute. Speak to no one about the matter, not even the reporters. I will take care of *them*; I will see that they get only what it may suit my ends to let them know.' He touched a bell; a youth appeared. 'Alaric, tell the reporters to remain for the present.' The boy retired.

'Now let us proceed to business – and systematically.

Nothing can be accomplished in this trade of mine without strict and minute method.'

He took a pen and some paper. 'Now – name of the elephant?'

'Hassan Ben Ali Ben Selim Abdallah Mohammed Moisé Alhammal Jamsetjejeebhoy Dhuleep Sultan Ebu Bhudpoor.'

'Very well. Given name?'

'Jumbo.'

'Very well. Place of birth?'

'The capital city of Siam.'

'Parents living?'

'No – dead.'

'Had they any other issue besides this one?'

'None. He was an only child.'

'Very well. These matters are sufficient under that head. Now please describe the elephant, and leave out no particular, however insignificant – that is, insignificant from *your* point of view. To men in my profession there *are* no insignificant particulars; they do not exist.'

I described – he wrote. When I was done, he said, 'Now listen. If I have made any mistakes, correct me.'

He read as follows:

'Height, 19 feet; length from apex of forehead to insertion of tail, 26 feet; length of trunk, 16 feet; length of tail, 6 feet; total length, including trunk and tail, 48 feet; length of tusks, 9 feet; ears in keeping with these dimensions;

footprint resembles the mark left when one up-ends a barrel in the snow; colour of the elephant, a dull white; has a hole the size of a plate in each ear for the insertion of jewellery, and possesses the habit in a remarkable degree of squirting water upon spectators and of maltreating with his trunk not only such persons as he is acquainted with, but even entire strangers; limps slightly with his right hind leg, and has a small scar in his left armpit caused by a former boil; had on, when stolen, a castle containing seats for fifteen persons, and a gold-cloth saddle-blanket the size of an ordinary carpet.'

There were no mistakes. The inspector touched the bell, handed the description to Alaric, and said, 'Have fifty thousand copies of this printed at once and mailed to every detective office and pawnbroker's shop on the continent.' Alaric retired. 'There – so far, so good. Next, I must have a photograph of the property.'

I gave him one. He examined it critically, and said, 'It must do, since we can do no better; but he has his trunk curled up and tucked into his mouth. That is unfortunate, and is calculated to mislead, for of course he does not usually have it in that position.' He touched his bell.

'Alaric, have fifty thousand copies of this photograph made, the first thing in the morning, and mail them with the descriptive circulars.'

Alaric retired to execute his orders. The inspector said,

'It will be necessary to offer a reward, of course. Now as to the amount?'

'What sum would you suggest?'

'To *begin* with, I should say – well, twenty-five thousand dollars. It is an intricate and difficult business; there are a thousand avenues of escape and opportunities of concealment. These thieves have friends and pals everywhere –'

'Bless me, do you know who they are?'

The wary face, practised in concealing the thoughts and feelings within, gave me no token, nor yet the replying words, so quietly uttered: 'Never mind about that. I may, and I may not. We generally gather a pretty shrewd inkling of who our man is by the manner of his work and the size of the game he goes after. We are not dealing with a pickpocket or a hall thief, now, make up your mind to that. This property was not "lifted" by a novice. But, as I was saying, considering the amount of travel which will have to be done, and the diligence with which the thieves will cover up their traces as they move along, twenty-five thousand may be too small a sum to offer, yet I think it worthwhile to start with that.'

So we determined upon that figure, as a beginning. Then this man, whom nothing escaped which could by any possibility be made to serve as a clue, said: 'There are cases in detective history to show that criminals have been detected through peculiarities in their appetites. Now, what does this elephant eat, and how much?'

'Well, as to *what* he eats – he will eat *anything*. He will eat a man, he will eat a Bible – he will eat anything *between* a man and a Bible.'

'Good – very good indeed, but too general. Details are necessary, details are the only valuable things in our trade. Very well – as to men. At one meal – or, if you prefer, during one day – how many men will he eat, if fresh?'

'He would not care whether they were fresh or not; at a single meal he would eat five ordinary men.'

'Very good; five men; we will put that down. What nationalities would he prefer?'

'He is indifferent about nationalities. He prefers acquaintances, but is not prejudiced against strangers.'

'Very good. Now, as to Bibles. How many Bibles would he eat at a meal?'

'He would eat an entire edition.'

'It is hardly succinct enough. Do you mean the ordinary octavo, or the family illustrated?'

'I think he would be indifferent to illustrations; that is, I think he would not value illustrations above simple letter-press.'

'No, you do not get my idea. I refer to bulk. The ordinary octavo Bible weighs about two pounds and a half, while the great quarto with the illustrations weighs ten or twelve. How many Doré Bibles would he eat at a meal?'

'If you knew this elephant, you could not ask. He would take what they had.'

'Well, put it in dollars and cents, then. We must get at

it somehow. The Doré costs a hundred dollars a copy, Russia leather, bevelled.'

'He would require about fifty thousand dollars' worth – say an edition of five hundred copies.'

'Now that is more exact. I will put that down. Very well; he likes men and Bibles; so far, so good. What else will he eat? I want particulars.'

'He will leave Bibles to eat bricks, he will leave bricks to eat bottles, he will leave bottles to eat clothing, he will leave clothing to eat cats, he will leave cats to eat oysters, he will leave oysters to eat ham, he will leave ham to eat sugar, he will leave sugar to eat pie, he will leave pie to eat potatoes, he will leave potatoes to eat bran, he will leave bran to eat hay, he will leave hay to eat oats, he will leave oats to eat rice, for he was mainly raised on it. There is nothing whatever that he will not eat but European butter, and he would eat that if he could taste it.'

'Very good. General quantity at a meal – say about –'

'Well, anywhere from a quarter to half a ton.'

'And he drinks –'

'Everything that is fluid. Milk, water, whiskey, molasses, castor oil, camphene, carbolic acid – it is no use to go into particulars; whatever fluid occurs to you set it down. He will drink anything that is fluid, except European coffee.'

'Very good. As to quantity?'

'Put it down five to fifteen barrels – his thirst varies; his other appetites do not.'

'These things are unusual. They ought to furnish quite good clues toward tracing him.'

He touched the bell. 'Alaric, summon Captain Burns.'

Burns appeared. Inspector Blunt unfolded the whole matter to him, detail by detail. Then he said in the clear, decisive tones of a man whose plans are clearly defined in his head, and who is accustomed to command, 'Captain Burns, detail Detectives Jones, Davis, Halsey, Bates, and Hackett to shadow the elephant.'

'Yes, sir.'

'Detail Detectives Moses, Dakin, Murphy, Rogers, Tupper, Higgins, and Bartholomew to shadow the thieves.'

'Yes, sir.'

'Place a strong guard – a guard of thirty picked men, with a relief of thirty – over the place from whence the elephant was stolen, to keep strict watch there night and day, and allow none to approach – except reporters – without written authority from me.'

'Yes, sir.'

'Place detectives in plain clothes in the railway, steamship, and ferry depots, and upon all roadways leading out of Jersey City, with orders to search all suspicious persons.'

'Yes, sir.'

'Furnish all these men with photograph and accompanying description of the elephant, and instruct them to search all trains and outgoing ferry-boats and other vessels.'

9

'Yes, sir.'

'If the elephant should be found, let him be seized, and the information forwarded to me by telegraph.'

'Yes, sir.'

'Let me be informed at once if any clues should be found – footprints of the animal, or anything of that kind.'

'Yes, sir.'

'Get an order commanding the harbour police to patrol the frontages vigilantly.'

'Yes, sir.'

'Despatch detectives in plain clothes over all the railways, north as far as Canada, west as far as Ohio, south as far as Washington.'

'Yes, sir.'

'Place experts in all the telegraph offices to listen to all messages; and let them require that all cipher despatches be interpreted to them.'

'Yes, sir.'

'Let all these things be done with the utmost secrecy – mind, the most impenetrable secrecy.'

'Yes, sir.'

'Report to me promptly at the usual hour.'

'Yes, sir.'

'Go!'

'Yes, sir.'

He was gone.

Inspector Blunt was silent and thoughtful a moment,

while the fire in his eye cooled down and faded out. Then he turned to me and said in a placid voice, 'I am not given to boasting, it is not my habit but – we shall find the elephant.'

I shook him warmly by the hand and thanked him; and I *felt* my thanks, too. The more I had seen of the man the more I liked him, and the more I admired him and marvelled over the mysterious wonders of his profession. Then we parted for the night, and I went home with a far happier heart than I had carried with me to his office.

2

Next morning it was all in the newspapers, in the minutest detail. It even had additions – consisting of Detective This, Detective That, and Detective The Other's 'Theory' as to how the robbery was done, who the robbers were, and whither they had flown with their booty. There were eleven of these theories, and they covered all the possibilities; and this single fact shows what independent thinkers detectives are. No two theories were alike, or even much resembled each other, save in one striking particular, and in that one all the eleven theories were absolutely agreed. That was, that although the rear of my building was torn out and the only door remained locked, the elephant had not been removed through the rent, but by some other (undiscovered) outlet. All agreed that the robbers had made that rent only to mislead the detectives. That never would have occurred to me or to any other layman, perhaps, but it had not deceived the detectives for a moment. Thus, what I had supposed was the only thing that had no mystery about it was in fact the very thing I had gone furthest astray in. The eleven theories all named the supposed robbers, but no two named the same robbers; the total number of suspected persons was thirty-seven. The various newspaper accounts all closed with the most important opinion of all – that of Chief Inspector Blunt. A portion of this statement read as follows:

The chief knows who the two principals are, namely, 'Brick' Duffy and 'Red' McFadden. Ten days before the robbery was achieved he was already aware that it was to be attempted, and had quietly proceeded to shadow these two noted villains; but unfortunately on the night in question their track was lost, and before it could be found again the bird was flown – that is, the elephant.

Duffy and McFadden are the boldest scoundrels in the profession; the chief has reasons for believing that they are the men who stole the stove out of the detective headquarters on a bitter night last winter – in consequence of which the chief and every detective present were in the hands of the physicians before morning, some with frozen feet, others with frozen fingers, ears, and other members.

When I read the first half of that I was more astonished than ever at the wonderful sagacity of this strange man. He not only saw everything in the present with a clear eye, but even the future could not be hidden from him. I was soon at his office, and said I could not help wishing he had had those men arrested, and so prevented the trouble and loss; but his reply was simple and unanswerable: 'It is not our province to prevent crime, but to punish it. We cannot punish it until it is committed.'

I remarked that the secrecy with which we had begun had been marred by the newspapers; not only all our facts but all our plans and purposes had been revealed; even all the suspected persons had been named; these would doubtless disguise themselves now, or go into hiding.

'Let them. They will find that when I am ready for them my hand will descend upon them, in their secret places, as unerringly as the hand of fate. As to the newspapers, we *must* keep in with them. Fame, reputation, constant public mention – these are the detective's bread and butter. He must publish his facts, else he will be supposed to have none; he must publish his theory, for nothing is so strange or striking as a detective's theory, or brings him so much wondering respect; we must publish our plans, for these the journals insist upon having, and we could not deny them without offending. We must constantly show the public what we are doing, or they will believe we are doing nothing. It is much pleasanter to have a newspaper say, "Inspector Blunt's ingenious and extraordinary theory is as follows," than to have it say some harsh thing, or, worse still, some sarcastic one.'

'I see the force of what you say. But I noticed that in one part of your remarks in the papers this morning you refused to reveal your opinion upon a certain minor point.'

'Yes, we always do that; it has a good effect. Besides, I had not formed any opinion on that point, anyway.'

I deposited a considerable sum of money with the inspector, to meet current expenses, and sat down to wait for news. We were expecting the telegrams to begin to arrive at any moment now. Meantime I reread the newspapers and also our descriptive circular, and observed that our $25,000 reward seemed to be offered only to detectives. I said I thought it ought to be offered to anybody who would catch the elephant. The inspector said: 'It is the detectives who will find the elephant, hence the reward will go to the right place. If other people found the animal, it would only be by watching the detectives and taking advantage of clues and indications stolen from them, and that would entitle the detectives to the reward, after all. The proper office of a reward is to stimulate the men who deliver up their time and their trained sagacities to this sort of work, and not to confer benefits upon chance citizens who stumble upon a capture without having earned the benefits by their own merits and labours.'

This was reasonable enough, certainly. Now the telegraphic machine in the corner began to click, and the following despatch was the result:

FLOWER STATION, N.Y., 7.30 A.M.
Have got a clue. Found a succession of deep tracks across a farm near here. Followed them two miles east without

result; think elephant went west. Shall now shadow him
in that direction.   DARLEY, *Detective*

'Darley's one of the best men on the force,' said the
inspector. 'We shall hear from him again before long.'
Telegram No. 2 came:

BARKER'S, N.J., 7.40 A.M.
Just arrived. Glass factory broken open here during night,
and eight hundred bottles taken. Only water in large quantity near here is five miles distant. Shall strike for there.
Elephant will be thirsty. Bottles were empty.

BAKER, *Detective*

'That promises well, too,' said the inspector. 'I told you
the creature's appetites would not be bad clues.'
Telegram No. 3:

TAYLORVILLE, L.I., 8.15 A.M.
A haystack near here disappeared during night. Probably
eaten. Have got a clue, and am off.

HUBBARD, *Detective*

'How he does move around!' said the inspector. 'I
knew we had a difficult job on hand, but we shall catch
him yet.'

FLOWER STATION, N.Y., 9 A.M.
Shadowed the tracks three miles westward. Large, deep,
and ragged. Have just met a farmer who says they are not
elephant tracks. Says they are holes where he dug up

saplings for shade-trees when ground was frozen last winter. Give me orders how to proceed.

DARLEY, *Detective*

'Aha! a confederate of the thieves! The thing grows warm,' said the inspector.

He dictated the following telegram to Darley:

Arrest the man and force him to name his pals. Continue to follow the tracks – to the Pacific, if necessary.

Chief BLUNT

Next telegram:

CONEY POINT, PA., 8.45 A.M.
Gas office broken open here during night and three months' unpaid gas bills taken. Have got a clue and am away. MURPHY, *Detective*

'Heavens!' said the inspector; 'would he eat gas bills?'

'Through ignorance – yes; but they cannot support life. At least, unassisted.'

Now came this exciting telegram:

IRONVILLE, N.Y., 9.30 A.M.
Just arrived. This village in consternation. Elephant passed through here at five this morning. Some say he went east, some say west, some north, some south – but all say they did not wait to notice particularly. He killed a horse; have secured a piece of it for a clue. Killed it with his trunk; from style of blow, think he struck it left-handed. From

position in which horse lies, think elephant travelled northward along line of Berkley railway. Has four and a half hours' start, but I move on his track at once.

HAWES, *Detective*

I uttered exclamations of joy. The inspector was as self-contained as a graven image. He calmly touched his bell.

'Alaric, send Captain Burns here.'

Burns appeared.

'How many men are ready for instant orders?'

'Ninety-six, sir.'

'Send them north at once. Let them concentrate along the line of the Berkley road north of Ironville.'

'Yes, sir.'

'Let them conduct their movements with the utmost secrecy. As fast as others are at liberty, hold them for orders.'

'Yes, sir.'

'Go!'

'Yes, sir.'

Presently came another telegram:

SAGE CORNERS, N.Y., 10.30 A.M.

Just arrived. Elephant passed through here at 8.15. All escaped from the town but a policeman. Apparently elephant did not strike at policeman, but at the lamp-post. Got both. I have secured a portion of the policeman as clue.

STUMM, *Detective*

'So the elephant has turned westward,' said the inspector. 'However, he will not escape, for my men are scattered all over that region.'

The next telegram said:

GLOVER'S, 11.15 A.M.
Just arrived. Village deserted, except sick and aged. Elephant passed through three quarters of an hour ago. The anti-temperance mass meeting was in session; he put his trunk in at a window and washed it out with water from cistern. Some swallowed it – since dead; several drowned. Detectives Cross and O'Shaughnessy were passing through town, but going south – so missed elephant. Whole region for many miles around in terror – people flying from their homes. Wherever they turn they meet elephant, and many are killed.   BRANT, *Detective*

I could have shed tears, this havoc so distressed me. But the inspector only said, 'You see – we are closing in on him. He feels our presence; he has turned eastward again.'

Yet further troublous news was in store for us. The telegraph brought this:

HOGANPORT, 12.19 P.M.
Just arrived. Elephant passed through half an hour ago, creating wildest fright and excitement. Elephant raged around streets; two plumbers going by, killed one – other escaped. Regret general.   O'FLAHERTY, *Detective*

19

'Now he is right in the midst of my men,' said the inspector. 'Nothing can save him.'

A succession of telegrams came from detectives who were scattered through New Jersey and Pennsylvania, and who were following clues consisting of ravaged barns, factories, and Sunday-school libraries, with high hopes – hopes amounting to certainties, indeed. The inspector said, 'I wish I could communicate with them and order them north, but that is impossible. A detective only visits a telegraph office to send his report; then he is off again, and you don't know where to put your hand on him.'

Now came this despatch:

BRIDGEPORT, CT., 12.15 P.M.
Barnum offers rate of $4,000 a year for exclusive privilege of using elephant as travelling advertising medium from now till detectives find him. Wants to paste circus-posters on him. Desires immediate answer.   BOGGS, *Detective*

'That is perfectly absurd!' I exclaimed. 'Of course it is,' said the inspector. 'Evidently Mr Barnum, who thinks he is so sharp, does not know me – but I know him.'

Then he dictated this answer to the despatch:

Mr Barnum's offer declined. Make it $7,000 or nothing.

Chief BLUNT

'There. We shall not have to wait long for an answer. Mr Barnum is not at home; he is in the telegraph office – it is his way when he has business on hand. Inside of three –'

Done. – P. T. BARNUM.

So interrupted the clicking telegraphic instrument. Before I could make a comment upon this extraordinary episode, the following despatch carried my thoughts into another and very distressing channel:

BOLIVIA, N.Y., 12.50 P.M.
Elephant arrived here from the south and passed through toward the forest at 11.50, dispersing a funeral on the way, and diminishing the mourners by two. Citizens fired some small cannonballs into him, and then fled. Detective Burke and I arrived ten minutes later, from the north, but mistook some excavations for footprints, and so lost a good deal of time; but at last we struck the right trail and followed it to the woods. We then got down on our hands and knees and continued to keep a sharp eye on the track, and so shadowed it into the brush. Burke was in advance. Unfortunately the animal had stopped to rest; therefore, Burke having his head down, intent upon the track, burred up against the elephant's hind legs before he was aware of his vicinity. Burke instantly rose to his feet, seized the tail, and exclaimed joyfully, 'I claim the re –' but got no further, for a single blow of the huge trunk laid the brave fellow's fragments low in death. I fled rearward, and the elephant turned and shadowed me to the edge of the wood,

making tremendous speed, and I should inevitably have been lost, but that the remains of the funeral providentially intervened again and diverted his attention. I have just learned that nothing of that funeral is now left; but this is no loss, for there is an abundance of material for another. Meantime, the elephant has disappeared again.

MULROONEY, *Detective*

We heard no news except from the diligent and confident detectives scattered about New Jersey, Pennsylvania, Delaware, and Virginia – who were all following fresh and encouraging clues – until shortly after 2 p.m., when this telegram came:

BAXTER CENTER, 2.15 P.M.

Elephant been here, plastered over with circus-bills, and broke up a revival, striking down and damaging many who were on the point of entering upon a better life. Citizens penned him up, and established a guard. When Detective Brown and I arrived, sometime after, we entered enclosure and proceeded to identify elephant by photograph and description. All marks tallied exactly except one, which we could not see – the boil-scar under armpit. To make sure, Brown crept under to look, and was immediately brained – that is, head crushed and destroyed, though nothing issued from debris. All fled; so did elephant, striking right and left with much effect. Has escaped, but left bold blood-track from cannon-wounds.

Rediscovery certain. He broke southward, through a dense forest.   BRENT, *Detective*

That was the last telegram. At nightfall a fog shut down which was so dense that objects but three feet away could not be discerned. This lasted all night. The ferry-boats and even the omnibuses had to stop running.

3

Next morning the papers were as full of detective theories as before; they had all our tragic facts in detail also, and a great many more which they had received from their telegraphic correspondents. Column after column was occupied, a third of its way down, with glaring headlines, which it made my heart sick to read. Their general tone was like this:

'THE WHITE ELEPHANT AT LARGE!

HE MOVES UPON HIS FATAL MARCH!

WHOLE VILLAGES DESERTED BY THEIR FRIGHT-
STRICKEN OCCUPANTS!

PALE TERROR GOES BEFORE HIM, DEATH AND
DEVASTATION FOLLOW AFTER!

AFTER THESE, THE DETECTIVES.

BARNS DESTROYED, FACTORIES GUTTED, HARVESTS
DEVOURED, PUBLIC ASSEMBLAGES DISPERSED,
ACCOMPANIED BY SCENES OF CARNAGE IMPOSSIBLE
TO DESCRIBE!

'There!' said Inspector Blunt, almost betrayed into excitement, 'this is magnificent! This is the greatest windfall that any detective organisation ever had. The fame of it will travel to the ends of the earth, and endure to the end of time, and my name with it.'

But there was no joy for me. I felt as if I had committed all those red crimes, and that the elephant was only my irresponsible agent. And how the list had grown! In one place he had 'interfered with an election and killed five repeaters.' He had followed this act with the destruction of two poor fellows, named O'Donohue and McFlannigan, who had 'found a refuge in the home of the oppressed of all lands only the day before, and were in the act of exercising for the first time the noble right of American citizens at the polls, when stricken down by the relentless hand of the Scourge of Siam.' In another, he had 'found a crazy sensation-preacher preparing his next season's heroic attacks on the dance, the theatre, and other things which can't strike back, and had stepped on him.' And in still another place he had 'killed a lightning-rod agent.' And so the list went on, growing redder and redder, and more and more heartbreaking. Sixty persons had been killed, and two hundred and forty wounded. All the accounts bore just testimony to the activity and devotion of the detectives, and all closed with the remark that 'three hundred thousand citizens and four detectives saw the dread creature, and two of the latter he destroyed.'

I dreaded to hear the telegraphic instrument begin to click again. By and by the messages began to pour in, but I was happily disappointed in their nature. It was soon apparent that all trace of the elephant was lost. The fog had enabled him to search out a good hiding place unobserved. Telegrams from the most absurdly distant points reported that a dim vast mass had been glimpsed there through the fog at such and such an hour, and was 'undoubtedly the elephant.' This dim vast mass had been glimpsed in New Haven, in New Jersey, in Pennsylvania, in interior New York, in Brooklyn, and even in the city of New York itself! But in all cases the dim vast mass had vanished quickly and left no trace. Every detective of the large force scattered over this huge extent of country sent his hourly report, and each and every one of them had a clue, and was shadowing something, and was hot upon the heels of it.

But the day passed without other result.

The next day the same.

The next just the same.

The newspaper reports began to grow monotonous with facts that amounted to nothing, clues which led to nothing, and theories which had nearly exhausted the elements which surprise and delight and dazzle.

By advice of the inspector I doubled the reward.

Four more dull days followed. Then came a bitter blow to the poor, hard-working detectives – the journalists declined to print their theories, and coldly said, 'Give us a rest.'

Two weeks after the elephant's disappearance I raised the reward to $75,000 by the inspector's advice. It was a great sum, but I felt that I would rather sacrifice my whole private fortune than lose my credit with my government. Now that the detectives were in adversity, the newspapers turned upon them, and began to fling the most stinging sarcasms at them. This gave the minstrels an idea, and they dressed themselves as detectives and hunted the elephant on the stage in the most extravagant way. The caricaturists made pictures of detectives scanning the country with spy-glasses, while the elephant, at their backs, stole apples out of their pockets. And they made all sorts of ridiculous pictures of the detective badge – you have seen that badge printed in gold on the back of detective novels, no doubt – it is a wide-staring eye, with the legend, '*We Never Sleep*.' When detectives called for a drink, the would-be facetious bar-keeper resurrected an obsolete form of expression and said, 'Will you have an eye-opener?' All the air was thick with sarcasms. But there was one man who moved calm, untouched, unaffected, through it all. It was that heart of oak, the Chief Inspector. His brave eye never drooped, his serene confidence never wavered. He always said, 'Let them rail on; he laughs best who laughs last.'

My admiration for the man grew into a species of worship. I was at his side always. His office had become an unpleasant place to me, and now became daily more and more so. Yet if he could endure it I meant to do so also; at least, as long as I could. So I came regularly, and stayed – the only outsider who seemed to be capable of it. Everybody wondered how I could; and often it seemed to me that I must desert, but at such times I looked into that calm and apparently unconscious face, and held my ground.

About three weeks after the elephant's disappearance, I was about to say one morning that I should *have* to strike my colours and retire, when the great detective arrested the thought by proposing one more superb and masterly move.

This was to compromise with the robbers. The fertility of this man's invention exceeded anything I have ever seen, and I have had a wide intercourse with the world's finest minds. He said he was confident he could compromise for $100,000 and recover the elephant. I said I believed I could scrape the amount together, but what would become of the poor detectives who had worked so faithfully? He said, 'In compromises they always get half.'

This removed my only objection. So the inspector wrote two notes, in this form:

DEAR MADAM – Your husband can make a large sum of money (and be entirely protected from the law) by making an immediate appointment with me.   *Chief* BLUNT

He sent one of these by his confidential messenger to the 'reputed wife' of Brick Duffy, and the other to the reputed wife of Red McFadden.

Within the hour these offensive answers came:

YE OWLD FOOL: brick McDuffys bin ded 2 yere.

BRIDGET MAHONEY

CHIEF Bat – Red McFadden is hung and in heving 18 month. Any Ass but a detective knose that.

MARY O'HOOLIGAN

'I had long suspected these facts,' said the inspector; 'this testimony proves the unerring accuracy of my instinct.'

The moment one resource failed him he was ready with another. He immediately wrote an advertisement for the morning papers, and I kept a copy of it:

A. – xwblv. 242 N. Tjnd – fz328wmlg. Ozpo – ; 2 m! ogw. MUM.

He said that if the thief was alive this would bring him to the usual rendezvous. He further explained that the usual rendezvous was a place where all business affairs between detectives and criminals were conducted. This meeting would take place at twelve the next night.

We could do nothing till then, and I lost no time in getting out of the office, and was grateful indeed for the privilege.

At 11 the next night I brought $100,000 in banknotes and put them into the chief's hands, and shortly afterward he took his leave, with the brave old undimmed confidence in his eye. An almost intolerable hour dragged to a close; then I heard his welcome tread, and rose gasping and tottered to meet him. How his fine eyes flamed with triumph! He said, 'We've compromised! The jokers will sing a different tune tomorrow! Follow me!'

He took a lighted candle and strode down into the vast vaulted basement where sixty detectives always slept, and where a score were now playing cards to while the time. I followed close after him. He walked swiftly down to the dim remote end of the place, and just as I succumbed to the pangs of suffocation and was swooning away he stumbled and fell over the outlying members of a mighty object, and I heard him exclaim as he went down, 'Our noble profession is vindicated. Here is your elephant!'

I was carried to the office above and restored with carbolic acid. The whole detective force swarmed in, and such another season of triumphant rejoicing ensued as I had never witnessed before. The reporters were called, baskets of champagne were opened, toasts were drunk, the hand-shakings and congratulations were continuous and enthusiastic. Naturally the chief was the hero of the hour, and his happiness was so complete and had been so patiently and worthily and bravely won that it made me happy to see it, though I stood there a homeless beggar, my priceless charge dead, and my position in my country's service lost to me through what would always seem my fatally careless execution of a great trust. Many an eloquent eye testified its deep admiration for the chief, and many a detective's voice murmured, 'Look at him – just the king of the profession – only give him a clue, it's all he wants, and there ain't anything hid that he can't find.' The dividing of the $50,000 made great pleasure; when it was finished the chief made a little speech while he put his share in his pocket, in which he said, 'Enjoy it, boys, for you've earned it; and more than that you've earned for the detective profession undying fame.'

A telegram arrived, which read:

Monroe, Mich., 10 p.m.
First time I've struck a telegraph office in over three weeks. Have followed those footprints, horseback, through the woods, a thousand miles to here, and they get stronger and bigger and fresher every day. Don't worry – inside of another week I'll have the elephant. This is dead sure.

Darley, *Detective*

The chief ordered three cheers for 'Darley, one of the finest minds on the force', and then commanded that he be telegraphed to come home and receive his share of the reward.

So ended that marvellous episode of the stolen elephant. The newspapers were pleasant with praises once more, the next day, with one contemptible exception. This sheet said, 'Great is the detective! He may be a little slow in finding a little thing like a mislaid elephant – he may hunt him all day and sleep with his rotting carcass all night for three weeks, but he will find him at last – if he can get the man who mislaid him to show him the place!'

Poor Hassan was lost to me forever. The cannon-shots had wounded him fatally, he had crept to that unfriendly place in the fog, and there, surrounded by his enemies and in constant danger of detection, he had wasted away with hunger and suffering till death gave him peace.

The compromise cost me $100,000; my detective expenses were $42,000 more; I never applied for a place again under my government; I am a ruined man and a wanderer in the earth – but my admiration for that man, whom I believe to be the greatest detective the world has ever produced, remains undimmed to this day, and will so remain unto the end.

The Story of the Bad Little Boy Who Didn't Come to Grief

Once there was a bad little boy, whose name was Jim – though, if you will notice, you will find that bad little boys are nearly always called James in your Sunday-school books. It was very strange, but still it was true, that this one was called Jim.

He didn't have any sick mother, either – a sick mother who was pious and had the consumption, and would be glad to lie down in the grave and be at rest, but for the strong love she bore her boy, and the anxiety she felt that the world would be harsh and cold toward him when she was gone. Most bad boys in the Sunday books are named James, and have sick mothers, who teach them to say, 'Now I lay me down,' etc., and sing them to sleep with sweet plaintive voices, and then kiss them goodnight, and kneel down by the bedside and weep. But it was different with this fellow. He was named Jim, and there wasn't anything the matter with his mother – no consumption, nor anything of that kind. She was rather stout than otherwise, and she was not pious; moreover, she was not anxious on Jim's account. She said if he were to break his neck, it wouldn't be much loss.

She always spanked Jim to sleep, and she never kissed him goodnight; on the contrary, she boxed his ears when she was ready to leave him.

Once this little bad boy stole the key of the pantry and slipped in there and helped himself to some jam, and filled up the vessel with tar, so that his mother would never know the difference; but all at once a terrible feeling didn't come over him, and something didn't seem to whisper to him, 'Is it right to disobey my mother? Isn't it sinful to do this? Where do bad little boys go who gobble up their good kind mother's jam?' and then he didn't kneel down all alone and promise never to be wicked anymore, and rise up with a light, happy heart, and go and tell his mother all about it, and beg her forgiveness, and be blessed by her with tears of pride and thankfulness in her eyes. No; that is the way with all other bad boys in the books; but it happened otherwise with this Jim, strangely enough. He ate that jam, and said it was bully, in his sinful, vulgar way; and he put in the tar, and said that was bully also, and laughed, and observed that 'the old woman would get up and snort' when she found it out; and when she did find it out, he denied knowing anything about it, and she whipped him severely, and he did the crying himself. Everything about this boy was curious – everything turned out differently with him from the way it does to the bad Jameses in the books.

Once he climbed up in Farmer Acorn's apple-tree to steal apples, and the limb didn't break, and he didn't fall and break his arm, and get torn by the farmer's great dog, and then languish on a sickbed for weeks, and repent and become good. Oh! no; he stole as many apples as he wanted, and came down all right; and he was all ready for the dog, too, and knocked him endways with a brick when he came to tear him. It was very strange – nothing like it ever happened in those mild little books with marbled backs, and with pictures in them of men with swallow-tailed coats, and bell-crowned hats, and pantaloons that are short in the legs, and women with the waists of their dresses under their arms and no hoops on. Nothing like it in any of the Sunday-school books.

Once he stole the teacher's penknife, and when he was afraid it would be found out, and he would get whipped, he slipped it into George Wilson's cap – poor Widow Wilson's son, the moral boy, the good little boy of the village, who always obeyed his mother, and never told an untruth, and was fond of his lessons and infatuated with Sunday-school. And when the knife dropped from the cap, and poor George hung his head and blushed, as if in conscious guilt, and the grieved teacher charged the theft upon him, and was just in the very act of bringing the switch down upon his trembling shoulders, a white-haired improbable justice of the peace did not suddenly appear in their midst and strike an attitude and say, 'spare this noble boy – there stands the cowering culprit! I was passing the school-door at recess, and, unseen myself, I saw the theft committed!' And then Jim didn't get whaled, and the venerable justice didn't read the tearful school a homily, and take George by the hand and say such a boy deserved to be exalted, and then tell him to come and make his home with him, and sweep out the office, and make fires, and run errands, and chop wood, and study law, and help his wife do household labours, and have all the balance of the time to play, and get forty cents a month, and be happy. No; it would have happened that way in the books, but it didn't happen that way to Jim. No meddling old clam of a justice dropped in to make trouble, and so the model boy George got thrashed, and Jim was glad of it; because, you know, Jim hated moral boys. Jim said he was 'down on them milksops.' Such was the coarse language of this bad, neglected boy.

But the strangest thing that ever happened to Jim was the time he went boating on Sunday and didn't get drowned, and that other time that he got caught out in the storm when he was fishing on Sunday, and didn't get struck by lightning. Why, you might look, and look, all through the Sunday-school books, from now till next Christmas and you would never come across anything like this. Oh! no; you would find that all the bad boys who go boating on Sunday invariably get drowned; and all the bad boys who get caught out in storms, when they are fishing on Sunday, infallibly get struck by lightning. Boats with bad boys in them always upset on Sunday, and it always storms when bad boys go fishing on the Sabbath. How this Jim ever escaped is a mystery to me.

This Jim bore a charmed life – that must have been the way of it. Nothing could hurt him. He even gave the elephant in the menagerie a plug of tobacco, and the elephant didn't knock the top of his head off with his trunk. He browsed around the cupboard after essence of peppermint, and didn't make a mistake and drink aqua fortis. He stole his father's gun and went hunting on the Sabbath, and didn't shoot three or four of his fingers off. He struck his little sister on the temple with his fist when he was angry, and she didn't linger in pain through long summer days, and die with sweet words of forgiveness upon her lips that redoubled the anguish of his breaking heart. No; she got over it. He ran off and went to sea at last, and didn't come back and find himself sad and alone in the world, his loved ones sleeping in the quiet churchyard, and the vine-embowered home of his boyhood rumbled down and gone to decay. Ah! no; he came home drunk as a piper, and got into the station house the first thing.

And he grew up, and married, and raised a large family, and brained them all with an axe one night, and got wealthy by all manner of cheating and rascality, and now he is the infernalest wickedest scoundrel in his native village, and is universally respected, and belongs to the Legislature.

So you see there never was a bad James in the Sunday-school books that had such a streak of luck as this sinful Jim with the charmed life.

The Story of the Good Little Boy
Who Did Not Prosper

[The following has been written at the insistence of several literary friends, who thought that if the history of 'The Bad Little Boy Who Didn't Come to Grief' (a moral sketch which I published five or six years ago) was worthy of preservation several weeks in print, a fair and unprejudiced companion piece to it would deserve a similar immortality. EDITORIAL MEMORANDUM]

Once there was a good little boy by the name of Jacob Blivens. He always obeyed his parents, no matter how absurd and unreasonable their demands were; and he always learned his book, and never was late at Sabbath school. He would not play hookey, even when his sober judgment told him it was the most profitable thing he could do. None of the other boys could ever make that boy out, he acted so strangely. He wouldn't lie, no matter how convenient it was. He just said it was wrong to lie, and that was sufficient for him. And he was so honest that he was simply ridiculous. The curious ways that that Jacob had surpassed everything. He wouldn't play marbles on Sunday, he wouldn't rob birds' nests, he wouldn't give hot pennies to organ-grinders' monkeys; he didn't seem to take any interest in any kind of rational amusement. So the other boys used to try to reason it out and come to an understanding of him, but they couldn't arrive at any satisfactory conclusion; as I said before, they could only figure out a sort of vague idea that he was 'afflicted,' and so they took him under their protection, and never allowed any harm to come to him.

This good little boy read all the Sunday-school books; they were his greatest delight. This was the whole secret of it. He believed in the good little boys they put in the Sunday-school books; he had every confidence in them. He longed to come across one of them alive, once; but he never did. They all died before his time, maybe. Whenever he read about a particularly good one, he turned over quickly to the end to see what became of him, because he wanted to travel thousands of miles and gaze on him; but it wasn't any use; that good little boy always died in the last chapter, and there was a picture of the funeral, with all his relations and the Sunday-school children standing around the grave in pantaloons that were too short, and bonnets that were too large, and everybody crying into handkerchiefs that had as much as a yard and a half of stuff in them. He was always headed off in this way. He never could see one of those good little boys, on account of his always dying in the last chapter.

Jacob had a noble ambition to be put in a

Sunday-school book. He wanted to be put in, with pictures representing him gloriously declining to lie to his mother, and she weeping for joy about it; and pictures representing him standing on the doorstep giving a penny to a poor beggar-woman with six children, and telling her to spend it freely, but not to be extravagant, because extravagance is a sin; and pictures of him magnanimously refusing to tell on the bad boy who always lay in wait for him around the corner, as he came from school, and welted him over the head with a lath, and then chased him home, saying 'Hi! hi!' as he proceeded. That was the ambition of young Jacob Blivens. He wished to be put in a Sunday-school book. It made him feel a little uncomfortable sometimes when he reflected that the good little boys always died. He loved to live, you know, and this was the most unpleasant feature about being a Sunday-school-book boy. He knew it was not healthy to be good. He knew it was more fatal than consumption to be so supernaturally good as the boys in the books were; he knew that none of them had ever been able to stand it long, and it pained him to think that if they put him in a book he wouldn't ever see it, or even if they did get the book out before he died, it wouldn't be popular without any picture of his funeral in the back part of it. It couldn't be much of a Sunday-school book that couldn't tell about the advice he gave to the community when he was dying. So, at last, of course he had to make up his mind to do the best he could under the circumstances – to live right, and hang on as long as he could, and have his dying speech all ready when his time came.

But somehow, nothing ever went right with this good little boy; nothing ever turned out with him the way it turned out with the good little boys in the books. They always had a good time, and the bad boys had the broken legs; but in his case there was a screw loose somewhere, and it all happened just the other way. When he found Jim Blake stealing apples, and went under the tree to read to him about the bad little boy who fell out of a neighbour's apple tree, and broke his arm, Jim fell out of the tree too, but he fell on *him*, and broke *his* arm, and Jim wasn't hurt at all. Jacob couldn't understand that. There wasn't anything in the books like it.

And once, when some bad boys pushed a blind man over in the mud, and Jacob ran to help him up and receive his blessing, the blind man did not give him any blessing at all, but whacked him over the head with his stick and said he would like to catch him shoving *him* again and then pretending to help him up. This was not in accordance with any of the books. Jacob looked them all over to see.

One thing that Jacob wanted to do was to find a lame dog that hadn't any place to stay, and was hungry and persecuted, and bring him home and pet him and have that dog's imperishable gratitude. And at last he found one, and was happy; and he brought him home and fed him, but when he was going to pet him the dog flew at him and tore all the clothes off him except those that were in front, and made a spectacle of him that was astonishing. He examined authorities, but he could not understand the matter. It was of the same breed of dogs that was in the books, but it acted very differently. Whatever this boy did, he got into trouble. The very things the boys in the books got rewarded for turned out to be about the most unprofitable things he could invest in.

Once when he was on his way to Sunday-school he saw some bad boys starting off pleasuring in a sailboat. He was filled with consternation, because he knew from his teaching that boys who went sailing on Sunday invariably got drowned. So he ran out on a raft to warn them, but a log turned with him and slid him into the river. A man got him out pretty soon, and the doctor pumped the water out of him and gave him a fresh start with his bellows, but he caught cold and lay sick abed nine weeks. But the most unaccountable thing about it was that the bad boys in the boat had a good time all day, and then reached home alive and well, in the most surprising manner. Jacob Blivens said there was nothing like these things in the books. He was perfectly dumbfounded.

When he got well he was a little discouraged, but he resolved to keep on trying, anyhow. He knew that so far his experiences wouldn't do to go in a book, but he hadn't yet reached the allotted term of life for good little boys, and he hoped to be able to make a record yet, if he could hold on till his time was fully up. If everything else failed, he had his dying speech to fall back on.

He examined his authorities, and found that it was now time for him to go to sea as a cabin boy. He called on a ship captain and made his application, and when the captain asked for his recommendations he proudly drew out a tract and pointed to the words: 'To Jacob Blivens, from his affectionate teacher.' But the captain was a coarse, vulgar man, and he said, 'Oh, that be blowed!' *That* wasn't any proof that he knew how to wash dishes or handle a slush-bucket, and he guessed he didn't want him. This was altogether the most extraordinary thing that ever had happened to Jacob in all his life. A compliment from a teacher, on a tract, had never failed to move the tenderest of emotions of ship captains and open the way to all offices of honour and profit in their gift – it never had in any book that ever *he* had read. He could hardly believe his senses.

This boy always had a hard time of it. Nothing ever came out according to the authorities with him. At last, one day, when he was around hunting up bad little boys to admonish, he found a lot of them in the old iron foundry fixing up a little joke on fourteen or fifteen dogs, which they had tied together in long procession and were going to ornament with empty nitroglycerine cans made fast to their tails. Jacob's heart was touched. He sat down on one of those cans – for he never minded grease when duty was before him – and he took hold of the foremost dog by the collar, and turned his reproving eye upon wicked Tom Jones. But just at that moment Alderman McWelter, full of wrath, stepped in. All the bad boys ran away; but Jacob Blivens rose in conscious innocence and began one of those stately little Sunday-school-book speeches which always commence with 'Oh, Sir!' in dead opposition to the fact that no boy, good or bad, ever starts a remark with 'Oh, Sir!' But the Alderman never waited to hear the rest. He took Jacob Blivens by the ear and turned him around, and hit him a whack in the rear with the flat of his hand; and in an instant that good little boy shot out through the roof and soared away toward the sun, with the fragments of those fifteen dogs stringing after him like the tail of a kite. And there wasn't a sign of that Alderman or that old iron foundry left on the face of the earth; and as for young Jacob Blivens, he never got a chance to make his last dying speech after all his trouble fixing it up, unless he made it to the birds; because, although the bulk of him came down all right in a treetop in an adjoining county, the rest of him was apportioned around among four townships, and so they had to hold five inquests on him to find out whether he was dead or not, and how it occurred. You never saw a boy scattered so.

Thus perished the good little boy who did the best he could, but didn't come out according to the books. Every boy who ever did as he did prospered, except him. His case is truly remarkable. It will probably never be accounted for.

The Celebrated Jumping Frog of Calaveras County

Mr A. Ward,

DEAR SIR: – Well, I called on good-natured, garrulous old Simon Wheeler, and I inquired after your friend Leonidas W. Smiley, as you requested me to do, and I hereunto append the result. If you can get any information out of it you are cordially welcome to it. I have a lurking suspicion that your Leonidas W. Smiley is a myth – that you never knew such a personage, and that you only conjectured that if I asked old Wheeler about him it would remind him of his infamous Jim Smiley, and he would go to work and bore me nearly to death with some infernal reminiscence of him as long and tedious as it should be useless to me. If that was your design, Mr Ward, it will gratify you to know that it succeeded.

I found Simon Wheeler dozing comfortably by the bar-room stove of the little old dilapidated tavern in the ancient mining camp of Boomerang, and I noticed that he was fat and bald-headed, and had an expression of winning gentleness and simplicity upon his tranquil countenance. He roused up and gave me good-day. I told him a friend of mine had commissioned me to make some inquiries about a cherished companion of his boyhood named Leonidas W. Smiley – Rev Leonidas W. Smiley – a young minister of the gospel, who he had heard was at one time a resident of this village of Boomerang. I added that if Mr Wheeler could tell me anything about this Rev Leonidas W. Smiley, I would feel under many obligations to him.

Simon Wheeler backed me into a corner and blockaded me there with his chair – and then sat down and reeled off the monotonous narrative which follows this paragraph. He never smiled, he never frowned, he never changed his voice from the quiet, gently-flowing key to which he tuned the initial sentence, he never betrayed the slightest suspicion of enthusiasm – but all through the interminable narrative there ran a vein of impressive earnestness and sincerity, which showed me plainly that so far from his imagining that there was anything ridiculous or funny about his story, he regarded it as a really important matter, and admired its two heroes as men of transcendent genius in finesse. To me, the spectacle of a man drifting serenely along through such a queer yarn without ever smiling was exquisitely absurd. As I said before, I asked him to tell me what he knew of Rev Leonidas W. Smiley, and he replied as follows. I let him go on in his own way, and never interrupted him once.

There was a feller here once by the name of *Jim* Smiley, in the winter of '49 – or maybe it was the spring of '50 – I don't recollect exactly, somehow, though what makes me think it was one or the other is because I remember the big flume wasn't finished when he first come to the camp; but anyway, he was the curiousest man about always betting on anything that turned up you ever see, if he could get anybody to bet on the other side, and if he couldn't he'd change sides – any way that suited the other man would suit *him* – any way just so's *he* got a bet, he was satisfied. But still, he was lucky – uncommon lucky; he most always come out winner. He was always ready and laying for a chance; there couldn't be no solitary thing mentioned but what that feller'd offer to bet on it – and take any side you please, as I was just telling you: if there was a horse race, you'd find him flush or you find him busted at the end of it; if there was a dogfight, he'd bet on it; if there was a catfight, he'd bet on it; if there was a chickenfight, he'd bet on it; why if there was two birds setting on a fence, he would bet you which one would fly first – or if there was a camp meeting he would be there reglar to bet on parson Walker, which he judged to be the best exhorter about here, and so he was, too, and a good man; if he even see a straddle-bug start to go anywheres, he would bet you how long it would take him to get wherever he was going to, and if you took him up he would foller that straddle-bug to Mexico but what he would find out where he was bound for and how long he was on the road. Lots of the boys here has seen that Smiley and can tell you about him. Why, it never made no difference to *him* – he would bet on *anything* – the dangdest feller. Parson Walker's wife laid very sick, once, for a good while, and it seemed as if they warn't going to save her; but one morning he come in and Smiley asked him how she was, and he said she was considerable better – thank the Lord for his inf'nit mercy – and coming on so smart that with the blessing of Providence she'd get well yet – and Smiley, before he thought, says, 'Well, I'll resk two and a half that she don't anyway.'

Thish-yer Smiley had a mare – the boys called her the fifteen-minute nag, but that was only in fun, you know, because, of course, she was faster than that – and he used to win money on that horse, for all she was so slow and always had the asthma, or the distemper, or the consumption, or something of that kind. They used to give her two or three hundred yards' start, and then pass her under way; but always at the fag-end of the race she'd get excited and desperate-like, and come cavorting and spraddling up, and scattering her legs around limber, sometimes in the air, and sometimes out to one side amongst the fences, and kicking up m–o–r–e dust, and raising m–o–r–e racket with her coughing and sneezing and blowing her nose – and always fetch up at the stand just about a neck ahead, as near as you could cipher it down.

And he had a little small bull-pup, that to look at him you'd think he warn't worth a cent, but to set around and look ornery, and lay for a chance to steal something. But

as soon as money was up on him he was a different dog –
his under-jaw'd begin to stick out like the for'castle of a
steamboat, and his teeth would uncover, and shine savage
like the furnaces. And a dog might tackle him, and
bully-rag him, and bite him, and throw him over his
shoulder two or three times, and Andrew Jackson – which
was the name of the pup – Andrew Jackson would never
let on but what he was satisfied, and hadn't expected
nothing else – and the bets being doubled and doubled
on the other side all the time, till the money was all up –
and then all of a sudden he would grab that other dog
just by the joint of his hind legs and freeze to it – not
chaw, you understand, but only just grip and hang on
till they throwed up the sponge, if it was a year. Smiley
always came out winner on that pup till he harnessed a
dog once that didn't have no hind legs, because they'd
been sawed off in a circular saw, and when the thing had
gone along far enough, and the money was all up, and
he came to make a snatch for his pet holt, he saw in a
minute how he'd been imposed on, and how the other
dog had him in the door, so to speak, and he 'peared
surprised, and then he looked sorter discouraged like,
and didn't try no more to win the fight, and so he got
shucked out bad. He gave Smiley a look as much as to
say his heart was broke, and it was *his* fault, for putting
up a dog that hadn't no hind legs for him to take holt of,
which was his main dependence in a fight, and then he
limped off a piece, and laid down and died. It was a good

pup, was that Andrew Jackson, and would have made a name for hisself if he'd lived, for the stuff was in him, and he had genius – I know it, because he hadn't had no opportunities to speak of, and it don't stand to reason that a dog could make such a fight as he could under them circumstances, if he hadn't no talent. It always makes me feel sorry when I think of that last fight of his'on, and the way it turned out.

Well, thish-yer Smiley had rat-terriers and chicken cocks, and tomcats, and all them kind of things, till you couldn't rest, and you couldn't fetch nothing for him to bet on but he'd match you. He ketched a frog one day and took him home and said he cal'lated to educate him; and so he never done nothing for three months but set in his back yard and learn that frog to jump. And you bet you he *did* learn him, too. He'd give him a little hunch behind, and the next minute you'd see that frog whirling in the air like a doughnut – see him turn one summerset, or maybe a couple, if he got a good start, and come down flat-footed and all right, like a cat. He got him up so in the matter of ketching flies, and kept him in practice so constant, that he'd nail a fly every time as far as he could see him. Smiley said all a frog wanted was education, and he could do most anything – and I believe him. Why, I've seen him set Dan'l Webster down here on this floor – Dan'l Webster was the name of the frog – and sing out, 'Flies! Dan'l, flies,' and quicker'n you could wink, he'd spring straight up, and snake a fly off'n the counter there, and flop down on the floor again as solid as a gob of mud, and fall to scratching the side of his head with his hind foot as indifferent as if he hadn't no idea he'd done any more'n any frog might do. You never see a frog so modest and straightfor'ard as he was, for all he was so gifted. And when it come to fair-and-square jumping on a dead level, he could get over more ground at one straddle than any animal of his breed you ever see. Jumping on a dead level was his strong suit, you understand, and when it come to that, Smiley would ante up money on him as long as he had a red. Smiley was monstrous proud of his frog, and well he might be, for fellers that had travelled and ben everywheres all said he laid over any frog that ever *they* see.

Well, Smiley kept the beast in a little lattice box, and he used to fetch him downtown sometimes and lay for a bet.

One day a feller – a stranger in the camp, he was – come across him with his box, and says: 'What might it be that you've got in the box?'

And Smiley says, sorter indifferent like, 'It might be a parrot, or it might be a canary, maybe, but it ain't – it's only just a frog.'

And the feller took it, and looked at it careful, and turned it round this way and that, and says, 'H'm – so 'tis. Well, what's *he* good for?'

'Well,' Smiley says, easy and careless, 'he's good enough for *one* thing I should judge – he can out-jump any frog in Calaveras county.'

The feller took the box again, and took another long, particular look, and give it back to Smiley and says, very deliberate, 'Well – I don't see no points about that frog that's any better'n any other frog.'

'Maybe you don't,' Smiley says. 'Maybe you understand frogs, and maybe you don't understand 'em; maybe you've had experience, and maybe you ain't only a amature, as it were. Anyways, I've got *my* opinion, and I'll resk forty dollars that he can out-jump any frog in Calaveras county.'

And the feller studied a minute, and then says, kinder sad, like, 'Well – I'm only a stranger here, and I ain't got no frog – but if I had a frog I'd bet you.'

And then Smiley says, 'That's all right – that's all right – if you'll hold my box a minute I'll go and get you a frog;' and so the feller took the box, and put up his forty dollars along with Smiley's, and set down to wait.

So he set there a good while thinking and thinking to hisself, and then he got the frog out and prised his mouth open and took a teaspoon and filled him full of quail-shot – filled him pretty near up to his chin – and set him on the floor. Smiley he went out to the swamp and slopped around in the mud for a long time, and finally he ketched a frog and fetched him in and give him to this feller and says:

'Now if you're ready, set him alongside of Dan'l, with his forepaws just even with Dan'l's, and I'll give the word.' Then he says, 'One – two – three – jump!' and him and the feller touched up the frogs from behind, and the new frog hopped off lively, but Dan'l give a heave, and hysted up his shoulders – so – like a Frenchman, but it wasn't no use – he couldn't budge; he was planted as solid as a anvil, and he couldn't no more stir than if he was anchored out. Smiley was a good deal surprised, and he was disgusted too, but he didn't have no idea what the matter was, of course.

The feller took the money and started away, and when he was going out at the door he sorter jerked his thumb over his shoulder – this way – at Dan'l, and says again, very deliberate, 'Well – *I* don't see no points about that frog that's any better'n any other frog.'

Smiley he stood scratching his head and looking down at Dan'l a long time, and at last he says, 'I do wonder what in the nation that frog throwed off for – I wonder if there ain't something the matter with him – he 'pears to look might baggy, somehow' – and he ketched Dan'l by the nap of the neck, and lifted him up and says, 'Why blame my cats if he don't weigh five pound' – and turned him upside down, and he belched out about a double-handful of shot. And then he see how it was, and he was the maddest man – he set the frog down and took out after that feller, but he never ketched him. And –

[Here Simon Wheeler heard his name called from the front yard, and got up to go and see what was wanted.] And turning to me as he moved away, he said: 'Just sit where you are, stranger, and rest easy – I ain't going to be gone a second.'

But by your leave, I did not think that a continuation of the history of the enterprising vagabond Jim Smiley would be likely to afford me much information concerning the Rev Leonidas W. Smiley, and so I started away.

At the door I met the sociable Wheeler returning, and he buttonholed me and recommenced: 'Well, this-yer Smiley had a yaller one-eyed cow that didn't have no tail only just a short stump like a bannanner, and –'

'O, curse Smiley and his afflicted cow!' I muttered, good-naturedly, and bidding the old gentleman good-day, I departed.

Yours, truly,

MARK TWAIN